SATURDAY

DENYS CAZET

Aladdin Books
Macmillan Publishing Company • New York
Collier Macmillan Publishers • London

For Bob Verrone

Aladdin Books
Macmillan Publishing Company
866 Third Avenue, New York, NY 10022
Collier Macmillan Canada, Inc.

First Aladdin Books edition 1988

Printed in the United States of America

A hardcover edition of *Saturday* is available from Bradbury Press, Macmillan Publishing Company.

10   9   8   7   6   5   4   3   2   1

Library of Congress Cataloging-in-Publication Data

Cazet, Denys.
  Saturday.

  Summary: Although Barney's day begins badly, Grandpa and Grandma soon find ways to make it all right again.
  [1. Dogs — Fiction. 2. Grandparents — Fiction]
I. Title.
PZ7.C2985Sat 1988   [E]   87-23883
ISBN 0-689-71065-8 (pbk.)

CONTENTS

GROUCH FROZEN

Barney smelled Grandma's pancakes.

He jumped out of bed and fell over the wastebasket. The basket bounced across the room and smashed his model airplane.

"Double ouch!" he shouted. "Three days at Grandma and Grandpa's house and this happens on the very first day!"

Barney picked up the airplane and looked at himself in the mirror. He stuck out his tongue.

He put on his shirt and went into the kitchen.

"Good morning," said Grandpa and Grandma.

Barney glared. "I've got the biggest grouches in the world!"

"Hummph!" snorted Grandpa, munching a fat pancake. "I've got to run errands all morning. Now there's a reason to have the grouches!"

"And mow the lawn," added Grandma.

"See?" said Grandpa. "My grouches

are a lot bigger than your grouches."

"I fell over the wastebasket and smashed my favorite airplane and I've got to do my school science project," grumbled Barney.

"And your shirt is inside out," added Grandma.

Barney folded his arms. *"My grouches are so big I'm grouch frozen!"*

"Grouch frozen?" repeated Grandpa. "Hear that, Grandma? Grouch frozen!"

Grandma nodded. She put a stack of steaming pancakes on the table. "Maybe these will melt the grouches."

Barney didn't move.

"Go on," urged Grandpa. "Eat one. If it doesn't melt your grouches, I'll eat my hat!"

Barney didn't move.

Grandma pushed the pancakes toward Barney's dish.

His nose twitched.

Grandma put her hands on her hips and raised her left eyebrow. She waited.

Grandpa stood up. He reached for his coat and tossed his cap onto the table.

"Those pancakes are the best grouch-melters I've ever eaten," he said. "My grouches are gone, vanished, invisibled, poofed."

Barney didn't move.

Grandpa picked up a big pancake and flopped it on his head.

"Good heavens!" cried Grandma, staring at the pancake.

"Grandpa!" shouted Barney.

"You don't have to shout," said Grandpa. "I'm going."

"But Grandpa . . ."

"Don't worry. I'll bring back a little surprise for both of you!"

"But Grandpa!" Barney pleaded. "Your cap!"

"What about it?" asked Grandpa. "This is my favorite cap. It's always nice and warm."

"Steamy," added Grandma, raising her right eyebrow.

Barney picked up Grandpa's cap from the table. "Look, Grandpa!"

"By gollies, I've got two caps!"

Barney laughed. "Grandpa, you're wearing a pancake!"

Grandpa took the pancake off his head. "No wonder it was so warm."

Barney climbed into his chair. He stabbed two pancakes with his fork.

Grandpa smiled at Barney. He plopped his pancake into a dish. "I thought you were grouch frozen!"

"Melted," Barney said. "Gone, vanished, invisibled—and poofed."

Grandma leaned on the table. "I thought you were running errands," she said.

"I am," said Grandpa, taking a bite of pancake. "But first, I think I'll eat my hat."

SURPRISES

Grandpa's old truck rattled into the driveway.

"Hi, Grandpa," Barney shouted. "Any surprises?"

"Can't remember," said Grandpa. "You better help me put all this stuff away, just in case there's something at the bottom that doesn't belong to Grandma or me."

Barney opened the door and took the packages from the seat.

He carried them upstairs. He helped Grandma put them away while Grandpa parked the truck in the garage.

Barney turned the last empty bag upside down. He couldn't find any surprises.

Grandpa peeked into the kitchen. "Surprise!" he shouted.

Grandpa handed Grandma a bouquet of flowers.

"You old cutie," she sighed. Grandma put the flowers in a vase.

Grandpa looked at Barney. "You're

not getting grouch frozen again, are you?"

"No," Barney said, looking at his shoes. "I was just . . . looking to see if my shoes were tied."

"Shoes!" snorted Grandpa. "Never mind your shoes. Take a look at this!"

Grandpa held up a long box he had
hidden behind his back.

"What is it?" asked Barney.

"It's a Triple-Whiz Rocket Plane."

"Double wow!" Barney yelled.

"Triple whiz wow!" said Grandpa.
"Let's fly it off the kitchen porch."

Grandma put her hands on her hips and raised her right eyebrow. "School work comes first! Barney has a science project to work on."

"This is science," Grandpa said. "And science marches on!"

"Right!" said Barney.

"Ten minutes!" said Grandma. "And then Little Science can march on downstairs and do his science project and Big Science can march onto the front lawn and mow it!"

Barney smelled Grandma's flowers. "They sure smell nice," he said.

Grandpa smiled.

"Fifteen minutes," said Grandma, rearranging the flowers.

Grandpa winked at Barney.

"Come on, Big Science," Barney said, slamming the screen door.

Grandpa put the rocket plane on the porch railing. "Flowers," he whispered. "It works every time."

"Right," said Barney.

CRASH LANDING

The Triple-Whiz Rocket Plane was ready.

"Stand back!" shouted Grandpa. "*Countdown!*"

"Ten, nine, eight, seven, six, five, four, three, two, one, *fire!*" Barney cried.

Grandpa fired the rocket plane. It roared into the air.

It swooshed higher and higher. It soared above the roof.

"Double wow!" yelled Barney, jumping up and down.

"Triple wow!" yelled Grandpa. "Now *that's* science!"

"Right!" said Barney.

The rocket plane sputtered. It stopped in midair and then sailed slowly down toward the ground.

"Oh oh!" said Grandpa.

"It's headed toward the Piggermans' house," Barney shouted. "Come on, Grandpa!"

They ran down the stairs and into the driveway.

"Look," Barney cried. "It's going toward the window."

The rocket plane flew gently through the open window and into the Piggermans' house.

"That was close!" said Grandpa,
peeking inside.

Mrs. Piggerman was taking a bath.

"*MISTER SPANIELSON!*" she cried.

Grandpa gasped.

"What's the matter, Grandpa?" asked Barney. "You look like you just saw the creature from Planet X."

"I think I did," gasped Grandpa again.

Mrs. Piggerman leaned out the window. A huge towel was wrapped around her. She handed Grandpa the rocket plane.

"I believe this is yours, Mr. Spaniel-son," Mrs. Piggerman said.

Grandpa pointed at Barney. "It's his."

"I'm sure!" smirked Mrs. Piggerman, slamming the window closed.

"Maybe you should give her some flowers," said Barney. "That works every time."

"Maybe I should go mow the lawn," said Grandpa, loosening his tie.

SCIENCE

Grandpa pushed the squeaky lawn-mower down the driveway and into the workshop.

Barney sat at the workbench twisting a long wire. "Hi, Grandpa."

Grandpa propped the mower against the wall. "What's that?"

"My school science project," Barney said. "It's an antenna for seeing creatures from outer space."

"Where's the rest of it?"

"I'm stuck, Grandpa." Barney shrugged. "I can't figure it out."

Grandpa held the wire in his hand. "Yep. I think it needs a little more zip at the top, and a lot more zap at the bottom."

"Like in the movie *Frankenstein?*" Barney asked.

"Exactly," nodded Grandpa.

Grandma leaned out the upstairs window. "Grandpa!" she shouted. "Did you finish trimming the lawn?"

"Can't," Grandpa called. "Got to help Barney with his school work. School work comes first you know."

"Well, hurry up. It's getting dark."

Grandpa gathered up odds and ends from the dusty room and piled them in the middle of the workbench.

"What is all that stuff?" Barney asked.

"Science," answered Grandpa. "Hand me that old radio."

Barney handed Grandpa the radio.

"Pliers."

Barney slapped the pliers into Grandpa's open hand.

"Pliers," repeated Barney.

"Screwdriver."

"Screwdriver," Barney said.

"Wrench."

"Wrench," Barney repeated again.

Grandpa fiddled with the project for a few more minutes and then stood back to admire his work. "What do you think?"

"More zip than a zipper!" said Barney.

"It's got zip," Grandpa said, "but not enough zap."

Grandpa plugged the electric cord into the wall socket.

"Careful, Grandpa," Barney warned.

Suddenly, the radio sputtered, sparks shot from the back and the lights went out with a loud crack!

"I think you blew a fuse, Grandpa."

"*MERCY ME!*" shouted Grandma. "*WHAT IS GOING ON DOWN THERE?*"

"Science," muttered Grandpa, striking a match. He opened the fuse box and screwed in a new fuse.

The lights went on.

"You boys come upstairs right now," Grandma called.

Barney unplugged the science project.

They carried the science project up the back stairs and went into the kitchen.

"Well?" said Grandma. "What were you two doing down there?"

"Grandpa was helping me put some zip and some zap into my science project," Barney said.

"Looks like the zap took the zip out of Grandpa," said Grandma, straightening his tie. "Go into the living room and I'll bring you two scientists some hot soup."

Grandpa and Barney went into the living room.

Barney pushed the science project up against the television and sat down next to Grandpa.

"Sorry," Grandpa said. "Looks like you won't be seeing any creatures from outer space tonight."

Barney jumped up. "And maybe I will," he laughed. "What time is it?"

Grandpa looked at his pocket watch. "Seven."

"Perfect," said Barney. "Help me put the television on top of our science project, Grandpa."

Barney and Grandpa moved the television set.

Barney bent the antenna on the science project. He adjusted the knobs on the old radio and turned on the television.

The screen flickered and a voice announced the Movie of the Week.

"The Creature from Planet X," said the television voice.

"My favorite," said Grandpa.

"See, Grandpa," Barney said, "I knew we could do it."

"By gollies," cried Grandpa, "you're right!"

Grandma brought in the hot soup. "Now what are you two up to?"

"We've contacted outer space," said Grandpa.

"See, Grandma?" said Barney. He pointed to the science project. It crackled and snapped.

Grandma looked at the science project. She looked at the television screen.

The creature from Planet X looked back.

"Mercy me," gasped Grandma.

THE CREATURE STRIKES

The creature from Planet X reached out toward the sleeping woman. Its long, thin suction-cup fingers curled over her face.

Suddenly the picture on the television screen changed. A smiling alligator appeared holding up a tube of toothpaste.

47

"Buy Allident," the smiling alligator said.

"By gollies!" shouted Grandpa. "Wouldn't you know it! Just when they're getting to the good part."

"This soup is the good part," said Grandma. "You'd better eat it before it gets cold."

"I wish I was an alligator," said Grandpa, taking out his false teeth. "I'd chew this guy up in a hurry!" Grandpa snapped his false teeth at the screen.

The television picture changed again. The creature from Planet X returned. It moved closer to the sleeping woman.

Grandpa leaned back in his chair.

"It's getting closer," gulped Barney.

"It looks like Mrs. Piggerman," Grandpa whispered. He put his false teeth on the edge of Grandma's rocking chair.

They fell onto the seat.

"Help, Grandpa!" Barney cried.

The creature touched the sleeping woman. Its eyes bulged.

Grandpa hung on to Barney.

"Really, you two!" Grandma said. "Eat your soup."

Just as the creature from Planet X grabbed the woman, Grandma sat down.

"*YEEOUCH!*" she screeched.

Grandpa jumped up from his chair and Barney landed on the floor.

"Something's biting me!" shouted Grandma.

"It's the creature from Planet X!" shouted Grandpa.

Grandma danced around the room. "Oh oh oh!" she cried.

Barney danced behind her and pulled off Grandpa's teeth with a loud snap.

"Suffering stinkweed!" Grandpa gasped. "You scared the bejabbers out of me!"

Barney held up Grandpa's teeth.

Grandma put her hands on her hips and stared at Grandpa. She raised both her eyebrows. "Put those things back where they belong!"

Grandma sat down. "Now finish your soup."

Except for Grandpa's slurping, it was quiet for a long time.

Suddenly, the television screen flickered again.

". . . And thank you for watching our Movie of the Week," said the alligator with the toothpaste. "Don't forget to brush before you bite. And when you brush, use Allident. Good night."

"Good night, Barney," said Grandma. "Time to go to bed."

"Already, Grandma?"

"Already," said Grandma. "The sooner you're in bed, the sooner Grandpa can come in and tell you a story."

"But what if I go to bed and get the grouches?" asked Barney. "What if I go to bed and get grouch frozen?"

"Grandma will make us some hot cocoa," Grandpa said. "Grandma's cocoa is famous for keeping the grouches away."

"Just like her pancakes," Barney said. He kissed Grandma goodnight.

"Don't forget to brush," said
Grandma.

Barney kissed Grandpa goodnight.

"See you later, alligator."

"Right." Grandpa smiled.

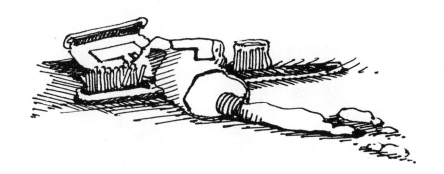

GOOD NIGHT!

Grandma set three cups of hot cocoa on the night stand.

"I'm ready," said Barney, fluffing up his pillow.

Grandpa sat down in an over-stuffed chair.

Grandma handed Barney a cup of cocoa.

"Double yum," said Barney, taking a sip. "Do I have a cocoa mustache?"

"Yes," said Grandma. "And it's almost as big as Grandpa's."

"Now you see it," Barney said, licking the mustache off, "and now you don't!"

"I remember when I lost my mustache," Grandpa said. "It was terrible."

"Did you shave it off by mistake?" Barney asked.

"Nope," said Grandpa, settling back in his chair. "It was stolen!"

"Stolen?" asked Barney.

"Stolen!" repeated Grandpa.

"But Grandpa!" Barney protested.
"How could . . ."

Grandpa raised his hand. "Do you
want to hear this story or don't you?"

"Right," said Barney.

"Then relax," said Grandpa. "Snuggle down and listen. Let your mind do the seeing and I'll do the talking."

Barney settled into the bed. He closed his eyes and opened his ears.

Grandpa started his story.

"Once upon a time, many, many years ago, before the time of Barney, when I was king of Spanielsonia and Grandma was queen . . ."

Grandma raised her left eyebrow. She tip-toed out of the bedroom and into the kitchen.

She washed the cocoa pot and put it away. She threw her dirty apron into the hamper and hung a clean one on a brass hook.

She peeked out at the stars before she closed the door.

The old house was quiet.

She tip-toed down the hall trying not to step on any creaky boards.

Grandma went into the bedroom.

Barney was asleep.

Grandpa snored softly in his chair.

Grandma took out an extra pillow and slipped it under Grandpa's head. She gently laid a blanket over him and tucked it under his chin.

She watched them for a few minutes
before she turned out the light.

"Good night, boys," she whispered.